RAINBOW
STREET
SHELTER

WANTED!
A Guinea Pig Called HENRY

The Rainbow Street Shelter Series

Lost! A Dog Called Bear

Missing! A Cat Called Buster

Wanted! A Guinea Pig Called Henry

Abandoned! A Lion Called Kiki

Stolen! A Horse Called Pebbles

Discovered! A Beagle Called Bella

RAINBOW
STREET
SHELTER

WANTED!
A Guinea Pig Called HENRY

by **Wendy Orr**

illustrations by **Patricia Castelao**

SQUARE
FISH

Henry Holt and Company   New York

SQUARE
FISH

An Imprint of Macmillan
175 Fifth Avenue
New York, NY 10010
mackids.com

Square Fish and the Square Fish logo are trademarks of Macmillan and
are used by Henry Holt and Company, LLC under license from Macmillan.

Square Fish books may be purchased for business or promotional use.
For information on bulk purchases, please contact the Macmillan Corporate
and Premium Sales Department at (800) 221-7945 x5442 or by e-mail
at specialmarkets@macmillan.com.

Library of Congress Cataloging-in-Publication Data
Orr, Wendy.
Wanted! A guinea pig called Henry / Wendy Orr ;
illustrations by Patricia Castelao.
p.   cm. — (Rainbow Street Shelter ; 3)
Summary: Sam chooses a guinea pig named Henry to be her pet, envisions a dog
named Nelly visiting and helping her younger brother Liam feel comfortable in
his kindergarten class, and encourages Liam to also get a guinea pig as a pet.
[1. Guinea pigs—Fiction. 2. Dogs—Fiction. 3. Brothers and sisters—Fiction.
4. Schools—Fiction.] I. Castelao, Patricia, ill. II. Title.
PZ7.O746Wan 2012   [Fic]—dc23   2011024413

ISBN 978-1-250-06273-4 (paperback)   ISBN 978-1-4299-4220-1 (ebook)

Originally published in the United States by Henry Holt and Company
First Square Fish Edition: 2015
Book designed by April Ward
Square Fish logo designed by Filomena Tuosto

10 9 8 7 6 5 4 3 2 1

AR: 4.7

For Suzie Q, Patty, Goofer . . .
and, of course, Henry

—W. O.

To all of Claudia's grandparents

—P. C.

1

When Nelly was a tiny, round brown puppy with short legs and a stumpy tail, she lived with a baby boy and his mother.

Nelly and the baby boy were always together. They rolled and tumbled across the floor and around the backyard. They played tug-of-war, splashed together in mud puddles, and dug in the sandbox.

When the baby boy cried, Nelly snuggled beside him, fussing over him as if she were a mother dog and he was her puppy.

But when the baby was a nearly two-year-old walking, talking little boy and

Nelly was an already grown-up dog, the mother got a new job in a country on the other side of the world. She and her little boy had to move, and they could not take Nelly with them.

The mother asked all her family and friends, but no one had a place for Nelly. There was only one thing she could do.

"We'll take her to the Rainbow Street Animal Shelter and ask them to find her a good home," the mother said.

Rainbow Street was short and narrow. At the end, surrounded by a tall wire fence, was a big garden with shady trees and green lawns. The building at its front was pale blue, with a bright rainbow arching over the cheery, cherry red door.

"Can I help you?" squawked a gray parrot as the little boy and his mother stepped into the waiting room with Nelly.

A young woman with long dark hair wound up above a kind face and a name tag that said MONA came out from a door. "Gulliver likes being the receptionist," she explained.

"Gulliver!" the parrot agreed, in his croaky old man's voice.

The mother smiled, and her little boy laughed.

But the little boy stopped laughing when his mother said good-bye to Nelly and lifted her into Mona's arms. He did not want to leave without his friend. He threw himself onto the floor, kicking and screaming in the loudest, most ferocious tantrum of his whole life.

With a wriggle and a squirm, Nelly leapt out of Mona's arms. She snuggled in tight against the little boy's side, licking the tears off his face until he had to giggle.

Then his mother picked him up, Mona picked up Nelly, and they said good-bye. The mother felt like crying, too, but she knew that this was the best place for the little stumpy-tailed dog to find a new home.

Mona met lots of dogs every day, but she

had never met one who worked so hard at making someone feel better.

"Now you need someone to look after you!" she said, when the little boy and his mother had gone. She stroked firmly down Nelly's back, one hand after the other, over and over, till the round brown body started to relax.

A gray-haired man came in from the dog runs, and smiled to see Mona sitting on the floor with the dog. He had never seen his busy friend look so relaxed.

"Will I take her out to a kennel now?" Juan asked gently. His voice was the same as the parrot's.

"*Hola, amigo!*" screeched Gulliver, flapping his wings with excitement.

"In a minute," said Mona, still stroking the little brown dog.

But before she could get up, the door burst open and a man came in carrying a white cat wrapped in a towel.

"She was running down the middle of the road, scared out of her wits!" the man said. "I don't know where she came from."

He put the cat bundle down on the floor.

Nelly leapt toward it.

The cat hissed, spat, and backed into a corner.

"Nelly!" shouted Mona.

"Sorry!" said the man.

"Can I help you?" screeched Gulliver.

"I think it's okay," said Juan—because
Nelly was not chasing the cat. Even when
she waved a scratching claw at Nelly's nose,
the little brown dog just crept forward on
her belly, her head down and bottom up,
stumpy tail wagging.

The white cat meowed but didn't hiss.
Nelly crept closer and started to lick
the frightened cat. The cat
twitched her tail in annoy-
ance, but let the dog
go on licking.

Finally, the cat gave a shake and jumped up onto the windowsill. She began smoothing her rumpled fur with her neat white paws, looking around the room as if she had always been there.

"I've never seen anything like that before!" said the man who'd rescued her.

"Neither have I," said Juan.

"Nelly," said Mona, "I think you've found your home."

So Nelly became Mona's dog, and came to the shelter with her every day.

The white cat stayed, too. No one ever came to find her, and she never wanted to leave the office. Juan named her Blanco, but even though Blanco loved Juan more than any other person, she never wanted to go home with him. She was happy just to curl up in her basket under the desk for the night.

In the morning, when Nelly and Mona came in, she rushed to greet them. Nelly licked her face till Blanco blinked and leapt up to her windowsill to wash the doggy kisses off her fur. For the rest of the day, she sat there watching everything that happened, letting people pat her if they asked politely, and keeping out of the way of the other dogs and cats as they came through the waiting room.

But Nelly liked meeting the people and animals that arrived feeling lost or worried. When puppies or kittens needed mothering, she stayed with them till they could be alone or were ready to be adopted. And if they were very young, Mona took them home at night so she could give them their midnight milk and Nelly could snuggle them all night long.

2

Sam had always wanted a pet. All her life she had thought she couldn't have one because her family lived in an apartment, high above the beach, and dogs and cats weren't allowed.

But the week before her birthday, when her mom asked her what sort of party she'd like, Sam said, "I don't need a party. I just want a pet."

"WHAT?" her mother and father both said at once, and so Sam said it again, because sometimes words didn't come out of her mouth the way they were supposed to, and she thought maybe she'd said something wrong.

Besides, Sam was so surprised herself at what came out of her mouth this time that she nearly said "WHAT?" too. She hadn't known she was going to ask for a pet: it was like a secret that her mind had been keeping even from her, and all of a sudden, it had to burst out and tell the truth.

"I know I can't have a dog or a cat," she said quickly, before her parents could say it. "But there are lots of other animals. Little animals that could live in an apartment and don't have to go for walks."

"What sort of little animal?" asked her mom.

"It would need a cage, whatever it is," said her dad. "You can't have something running wild around the apartment."

"But it's still a whole week before my birthday," said Sam. "Couldn't we just go to the pet store and look?"

Her parents looked at each other. Sam knew that look.

"Please?" she begged. "I promise I won't ask to buy anything today."

"Is there even a pet store around here?" her dad asked.

"No," said her mom. "But there's the animal shelter on Rainbow Street."

Her dad went to get the car keys.

Sam could never jump very high, but inside she was leaping like a rabbit who'd found a brand-new carrot patch.

The first animal that Sam and her family saw, before they even got into the shelter, was a three-legged goat grazing on the lawn.

"Oh, the poor thing!" exclaimed Sam's mom.

"Can we take him home?" asked Sam's little brother.

"Goats don't live in apartments, Liam," said their dad. "He'd eat the curtains!"

Sam liked that this goat didn't seem to mind that he didn't have as many legs as other goats, and she smiled at him as they walked up the path.

They all went in the cheery, cherry red door under the bright painted rainbow.

Mona was at the desk, with a framed photograph of a lion and two cubs behind her. Gulliver was on his perch, watching the Ballarts as they came into the waiting room.

Gulliver and Mona both said at once, "Can I help you?"

"We'd like to see some small animals," said Sam's mom.

"Just to get some ideas," said her dad. "We don't want to take a pet home today."

Sam hardly heard them. A warm buzz of happiness was thrilling through her because a little brown stumpy-tailed dog was sniffing her legs and a white cat was sitting in the windowsill, washing her face with neat white paws. Sam knew that all around her were animals needing someone to love and needing someone to love them back.

"No problem!" Gulliver screeched, in Mona's voice.

Maybe I could have a bird, Sam thought.

But Gulliver looked as if he belonged here, and he didn't look as if he needed someone to love and cuddle him. He sounded as if he liked being the boss, and he made Sam feel a bit nervous. She wanted a little friend who needed to be patted and played with and didn't tell her what to do.

"The bunnies are mostly outside," said Mona, "but the other ones you might like to see are in here." She opened a door marked SMALL ANIMAL ROOM.

Liam squatted down to talk to the little brown dog, but Sam and her mother and father followed Mona into the room.

"Hi, guys," Mona said, looking around at the cages and hutches against the walls. "You've got visitors."

Mr. and Mrs. Ballart looked surprised.

"They don't understand exactly what

I'm saying," Mona admitted. "But it only seems fair to tell them what's happening. Animals like being talked to, just like us."

Sam hugged Mona's words inside herself. When she had her own pet, she would talk to it every day. She would tell it all her secrets, and it would never let them go. And whatever she said, her pet would never laugh if the words didn't come out right.

3

Sam was almost glad she'd promised not to ask to take a pet home today.

There were so many animals in the room, and they were all so cute, that she'd never have been able to decide. There were gerbils in cages on their own, hamsters in pairs, and one brown-and-white hamster running endlessly in his plastic wheel.

There were white rats and piebald mice. There was a blond guinea pig mother with three tiny blond babies.

"The babies won't be ready to leave their mom for another week," said Mona.

Mona talked quietly to all the animals as she handled them. She showed Sam how to put her hand in a gerbil's cage and wait till the little animal trusted her enough to climb into her palm and nibble the celery she was holding.

"Just stay like that," said Mona. "He'll be a bit nervous this first time, and he might hurt himself if he jumps out of your hand onto the floor."

As soon as she said "jumps," the gerbil leapt out of Sam's hand and raced across to the other side of his cage, as if he'd had enough of talking to people for one day.

One by one, Mona showed Sam how to hold the other small animals. Sam held a hamster, two mice, and a rat. She patted the guinea pig mother and held one of the babies in her hand, but the mother looked around so anxiously that Sam put the baby back before Mona asked her to.

By the time they said good-bye to the animals, Sam's head was whirling with trying to remem- ber all the things Mona had told her.

They went back to the waiting room, where Liam was still sitting with the brown stumpy-tailed dog.

"I'm going to school soon," he was telling her. "I'm a big boy now. I'm going to learn to read, and I'll have lots of friends and do *everything!*"

Mona smiled. "I see you've found a new friend," she said to Liam. "Nelly loves everyone—both animals and people—but I think she really misses having little kids in her life."

Liam hugged the round brown dog good-bye.

"You know," Mona said gently, "not all dogs are as friendly as Nelly. You shouldn't hug dogs you don't know."

"Nelly," said Liam, "my name is Liam." And he hugged the dog again.

Sam would have liked to hug Nelly, too, but she wasn't sure if she should after what Mona had said, so she just patted the smooth brown head.

"Go ahead and hug her," said Mona. "Nelly loves it. I just wanted your little brother to understand that not all dogs are like that."

Sam hugged the dog, and the warmth of the solid brown body melted away the muddle of wondering what pet she should choose and how. She didn't know what sort of animal was going to be right for her, but she was starting to believe there would be one.

As they left, Mona handed Sam a bundle of leaflets. "These will tell you more about the different kinds of animals you met today and how to look after them. And don't forget—you can come back any time and have another look. You'll know when you've found the animal that's right for you."

Nelly stood at the door to watch the Ballarts leave.

"You liked that little boy, didn't you?" Mona asked, rubbing behind Nelly's ears. "But they can't have a dog, and I couldn't do without you."

Nelly snuggled up against Mona. No matter how much she liked children, she knew that she and Mona belonged together, and she never wanted to go anywhere else.

4

Now Sam had three things to be excited about. In six more days, it would be her birthday, and she'd go back to Rainbow Street to choose her pet. And two days after that, school would start.

Sam never told anyone that she was excited about going back to school. She knew her friends would say that was weird.

But Sam liked school. She didn't like gym classes, because her arms and legs didn't always do exactly what she told them, and she didn't like being teased by other kids because of that. What she liked was figuring out new things, like in her science extension classes—because Sam's brain was one part of her that worked just fine. And her best friends knew that and understood when words didn't come out the way they were supposed to.

Still, part of Sam would have liked to be able to run fast along the beach or jump high to catch a ball. When she watched her little brother run and jump, she hugged it like a secret inside her. Liam was going to be happy at school right from the start.

He wouldn't get laughed at or teased by bullies because he could run fast, jump high, and catch any ball, no matter who threw it.

She didn't tell her friends that either. Everyone knew that little brothers were a pain, and sometimes Liam was. But Sam was still excited about how happy he was going to be at school.

In the corner of the small animal room, Henry gave a lonesome whistle. His hutch was filled with clean shredded paper that was soft against his fur. He had water to drink and hay to eat—but he was tired and confused. Three weeks ago, he'd been

living in a pet shop with lots of other guinea pigs. A boy had come in, tied a ribbon around Henry's belly, and taken him to a party with lots of other boys and lots of noise.

"What is it?" asked the birthday boy, who had never met a guinea pig before. Even when he found out, he didn't really want one, so his father had picked up the cardboard box with Henry inside and dropped it off at the Rainbow Street Shelter.

Sam and her parents read all the information sheets that Mona had given them, but they still couldn't decide which animal would be the best pet.

They learned that hamsters like to sleep in the day and sometimes get grumpy if they're woken up; that gerbils are happier if there are two of them, but they need to be from the same litter; and that rats can learn to do tricks.

Mrs. Ballart worried that rabbits needed too much room, and Mr. Ballart worried that the fancy mice might escape.

Sam's mind was running in circles and getting nowhere, exactly like the brown-and-white hamster in his wheel.

"Don't worry," said her mom, when she kissed Sam good night. "It'll turn out okay, no matter what you choose."

Sam tried to smile, but she almost wished that she had never asked for a pet if it was going to be this hard to decide!

That night, she dreamed of cuddling an animal with soft, thick hair. It was small but solid and sat quietly on her lap. It wasn't any of the animals that she'd actually held at the shelter.

"I want a guinea pig," Sam said when she woke up in the morning. A quiet bubble of happiness was swelling inside her, and she knew she was right.

She remembered the mother guinea pig with the little blond babies. "They'll be ready to leave their mother in another week," Mona had said. That meant Sam could take one of the babies home on her birthday!

She would choose a girl baby, and she'd name it SugarSpice. The name just popped into her head, and Sam knew that was another sign that this was going to come true.

"Then the first thing to do," said her dad, "is build a guinea pig cage."

So right after breakfast, Sam went to the computer and searched for a plan. She printed it out and then she and her dad went to the hardware store and bought everything they needed for SugarSpice's home.

They built the hutch to fit into the hall between Sam's and Liam's bedrooms, so

it was longer than the plan said. It was magnificent. It was a guinea pig palace.

It had a solid plastic bottom that would be easy to clean and wire grid sides so SugarSpice would be able to see everything going on around her, but couldn't climb out. At one end there was a ramp up to the second story. The second story had a plastic floor and wire grid sides too, but it was only half as long as the bottom.

They put shredded paper on the floor, and finally they put in the wooden bedroom box, on the bottom floor so the guinea pig could find it easily. The box had one side open for a door and a window cut out on each side. Sam imagined how she would peek in to see SugarSpice asleep in her bedroom.

When she tried to imagine holding SugarSpice, it didn't feel exactly like the solid little animal in her dream, but she knew that a baby guinea pig would grow and soon be just the way she pictured.

Sam had five more days to wait.

"Could we go back and visit?" Sam asked her parents, but the weekend was over and they were busy.

"And you can't take it home any sooner," said her mom. "You know Mona said it was still a week before they could leave the mother."

"Just wait till your birthday," said her dad. "It'll be there."

Sam's mom said that she could still have a party, so Sam wrote invitations to her three best friends to come to her house on Saturday afternoon for a HAPPY

BIRTHDAY TO SAM AND WELCOME TO SUGARSPICE party.

And then she waited. She went to the library and found a book about looking after guinea pigs. She drew pictures for the walls of the cage and made up a guinea pig rhyme:

Guinea pig, guinea pig,
You're so nice.
That's why I call you
Sweet SugarSpice.

Late on Friday afternoon, Mona brought a girl to the small animal room to meet

Henry. The girl lifted the guinea pig out of his cage to hold him against her shoulder. Henry wiggled and sniffed her ponytail. But before he could decide whether she was a safe person to trust, the girl put him back in his cage. Henry was alone again.

The night before her birthday, Sam dreamed another guinea pig dream. Sugar-Spice was all grown up, because she was warm and solid on Sam's lap, and her fur had turned from blond to black. *Dreams are funny!* Sam thought when she woke up.

But the strongest thing in the dream was the warm honey feeling of happiness, just sitting and stroking her animal friend. That was the part she knew was true.

So right after breakfast, when Sam had opened the guinea pig card that Liam had drawn and the guinea pig book that her parents had bought, the whole family went to the Rainbow Street Shelter.

"Can I help you?" shrieked the parrot.

Liam threw his arms around the little brown dog and started telling her all about getting ready to go to school on Tuesday.

Mona came out of the small animal room, and Sam rushed in.

The hutch with the blond guinea pig mother and her three babies was empty.

SugarSpice wasn't there.

5

"Someone wanted the mother as well as the babies, so we didn't have to wait," Mona said to Sam's parents. "Guinea pigs are always happier when they've got company, even when they're grown up."

Mr. and Mrs. Ballart looked at each other sadly. They knew how upset Sam was going to be if she couldn't have her

44

blond guinea pig baby. Her whole birthday was ruined.

But Sam wasn't listening—because there, in another hutch in the corner, was the guinea pig from her dream.

He was fat, black, and whiskery. Sam squatted down beside him.

"Hello, Henry," she said.

"Are you sure?" asked her mother. "I thought you wanted a baby one."

"A pet has to be the right one for you," said Mona.

"He's the absolutely perfect one," said Sam.

Mona smiled and put Henry into Sam's waiting hands. He felt exactly like he had in the dream: soft, warm, and solid. His black hair was shaggy, and his whiskers stuck out as if he hadn't had time to brush his hair this morning. He was the cutest guinea pig Sam had ever seen.

In fact, he was the cutest pet she had ever seen. He was so cute that Sam was suddenly sure there was a mistake and that he already belonged to someone else.

"Does he need a home?" she asked. The words came out fine, but her voice was quivery.

"I think he's just found one," Mona said.

Sam's birthday/Henry's welcome party wasn't big, but it was absolutely perfect. Her three best friends were there, and Liam and her parents . . . and Henry.

Sam carried Henry around so he could see everywhere in the apartment. She introduced him to her friends and let them pat him. But Mona had said to let him have some time to get used to his new home, so when everyone had said hello,

Sam put him into the guinea pig palace she and her dad had built.

Henry was very quiet. He scurried around his shredded paper bedding. He had a drink from his water bottle and ate some hay. Then he went into his wooden bedroom box. Sam peeked through the little window, but she couldn't tell if he was asleep or just resting.

After Sam's friends had gone home, though, when her parents were in the kitchen and Liam had gone to bed, Henry came out.

"Hi, there, Henry," Sam murmured. "Are you hungry?"

She held out a piece of celery. Henry

came closer. He was still shy, but he wanted that celery.

Finally he came close enough to nibble at the leaves. Sam kept holding the stem.

"Yum, yum, celery!" said Sam. She didn't mind what she said to Henry because she knew Henry would listen to what she meant, and what she meant was that she was his friend.

Henry's nose wiggled, his cheeks puffed, and his teeth crunched as fast as they could. The celery disappeared right up to the last inch in Sam's fingers.

"Do you want some carrot now?" Sam asked, and went to the kitchen to get it.

When she came back, Henry was not

being quiet at all. He was exploring his cage, chirping and whistling, up the ramp to the top floor and down again, hopping like popcorn in a hot pan.

Henry was a very happy guinea pig.

Maybe Mona was wrong, Sam thought. Maybe most guinea pigs liked to have other guinea pigs for company—but Henry just needed Sam.

All the rest of that day, Nelly had wagged her stumpy tail at the people and pets who came in. She'd gone out to the runs in the back yard to sniff noses with the dogs that were waiting to find homes. She'd let a lost border collie bounce all around her until he felt calmer again, but Mona knew that something wasn't quite right.

"How about we go to the beach on our way home?" Mona said, and Nelly pricked up her floppy ears.

Nelly liked the beach. It had soft sand to dig in and shallow waves to run in, but best of all, it had children. Kids who talked to her, kids who threw her a ball, kids who stroked her head and rubbed her freckled pink tummy when she rolled onto her back.

She led Mona past one group of kids after another, collecting pats and love until her round brown eyes were glowing with happiness.

"Oh, Nelly," sighed Mona, as the little dog settled happily onto the backseat on the way home. "I'm sorry I don't know any kids for you to visit."

6

Liam was very excited about going to school with his big sister, but when he found out that Sam wasn't going to stay with him, his lip started to quiver.

"You'll make lots of friends!" said their mom, and hugged him again as Sam waved good-bye.

Sam was excited, too. She knew her words would come out just right when it was her turn to stand up and say to the class, "The most exciting thing I did this summer was get a guinea pig from the Rainbow Street Animal Shelter."

It was nearly her turn when a bouncy ponytailed girl called Hannah stood up and said, "Last Friday my dad came home with a dog in the back of his truck. It's got shaggy black fur, a white neck, three white paws, and a really cute floppy white ear."

That sounds like a dog I saw at the shelter! Sam thought, but at the same moment, the new boy in front of her jumped to his feet so fast his desk tipped over.

"His name is Bear!" Logan shouted.

The teacher decided to stop the Going-Around-the-Room-Telling-About-Last-Summer so they could sort out the mystery of whether it was really Logan's lost dog and how it had ended up in Hannah's dad's truck.

Sam couldn't imagine how she'd feel if Henry got lost. She understood how disappointed Logan felt when the teacher said he had to wait till after school to go to Rainbow Street to find his dog.

By the time the teacher asked Sam to tell her summer story, she was afraid that her words wouldn't come out right after all, because getting a guinea pig from the shelter wasn't quite as exciting as a lost-and-found-dog mystery.

But when she told it, the teacher said, "It sounds like the Rainbow Street Shelter was a busy place last weekend!"

Hannah turned around and smiled at her, her ponytail swinging. "I'm glad!" she whispered.

"So am I!" Sam whispered back.

Liam's day hadn't been nearly as good.

"Did you make any friends?" Sam asked.

Liam shook his head. "There are too many kids!" he said. "I don't want to talk to so many kids!"

"You'll get used to it," said Sam, but she felt sad. She wanted her little brother to be happy and brave at school right from the start.

That night, Liam showed his reader to his mom and told her the story. He could already read a few words because of the stories his parents and Sam read him at home.

"Your teacher's going to be very pleased with you!" said their mom.

"There are too many kids!" Liam said again. "I'm not going to say the book at school!"

Sam was suddenly so angry she thought she was going to burst like a too-big balloon. Liam could talk so well and do everything so easily—it wasn't fair if he just didn't bother!

She picked up Henry and marched to her bedroom. She wanted to slam the door with a great, angry bang, but she didn't want to scare Henry.

The guinea pig sat quietly on her lap, just like he had in her dream. She held

him up to her shoulder so his furry head
tickled her neck.

It's hard to be angry when you're holding a fat, furry guinea pig.

And once you stop being horribly, boiling-red furious, it's hard not to laugh when that fat, furry guinea pig tickles your neck.

Sam went to get an apple from the fridge, shutting her bedroom door behind her. When she came back, Henry had disappeared.

"Henry!" Sam called softly. "Henry, where are you?" She wasn't sure if he was supposed to be loose in her bedroom, and she didn't want her mom to know that she couldn't find him.

After a moment, she heard a rustling under her bed. Sam lay down on the floor and looked into a pair of bright eyes.

"Hey, there," she whispered.

Henry stared back.

Sam rolled the red apple to the edge of the bed. Henry came closer. Sam shoved it gently toward him till the apple was nearly touching his nose.

Henry crept forward. He tried to bite the apple, and it rolled out from under the bed. Nudge by nudge and nibble by nibble, Henry rolled the apple to the middle of the room. Sam sat quietly and watched him. When the apple rolled toward her, she pushed it gently back to the guinea pig.

By the time her mom called her for dinner, the apple had rolled back and forth and around the room five times. Now it was resting against her desk and Henry was nibbling white chunks out of its red skin. Sam moved quietly toward him and picked him up.

"Thank you, Henry," she whispered, because she'd been a bit worried she might not be able to catch him. She snuggled him close for a second and put him back in his cage.

"Samantha!" her mother called again.

Sam got a tissue and quickly picked up a few little black pellets from the floor. She flushed them down the toilet, washed her hands, and raced to the kitchen.

Her mom was already sitting at the table, but Sam hugged her tight. "Henry's the best present *ever*," she said.

"I'm glad," said her dad, and Sam hugged him, too.

"I love Henry," said Liam, and Sam couldn't be angry at him anymore.

She brought Henry out of his cage again after dinner and let Liam hold him.

7

Sometimes Sam wished she could let Liam take Henry to school because holding the guinea pig made her feel good, no matter what else was wrong, and she knew he made Liam happy, too. But even if guinea pigs were allowed to go to school, Henry wouldn't like being in the middle of a bunch of noisy kids any more than Liam did.

Friday was a hot fall day, and after work and school, the whole Ballart family went to the beach. Sam almost didn't want to go, because she'd been away from Henry all day at school, and it would mean leaving him alone again now.

"Come on, Sam!" called her dad. "You can't stay home on your own."

"Henry will be fine," added her mom.

The guinea pig's whiskery black face stared at her. She knew he was saying, "It's time for me to play outside the cage!"

"We'll play the apple game when I get back," Sam promised.

Henry kept on staring . . . and then he whistled—but when he heard the door shut, he knew he was alone again.

It was warm enough that even Mr. Ballart went for a swim. Liam splashed, and their mom swam back and forth between the flags, but Sam stayed in the water the longest, jumping over the little waves and catching the bigger ones on her boogie board until she was tired and shivery.

Liam was already wrapped in his towel when she came out.

"Look!" he shouted suddenly.

Mona and Nelly were splashing along the water's edge.

Liam raced across the sand and threw his arms around the little brown dog. Nelly licked his face, Mr. and Mrs. Ballart came over to get Liam, and Mona laughed.

"How's the guinea pig?" Mona asked Sam.

"He whistles a lot," said Sam, "and he jumps around his cage."

"Then he's happy," said Mona.

Sam felt so warm she stopped shivering. If Mona said he was happy, Sam didn't have to feel guilty that he didn't have a guinea pig friend.

"I can read, too!" Liam was telling Nelly. "Do you want me to tell you the story?"

The little dog snuggled against him as if she was saying yes, and Liam told her the story from his reader the night before.

"Why doesn't he do that at school?" Sam asked her dad. "It's so easy for him!"

"It doesn't matter how good people are at things," said her dad. "They still have to get up the nerve to do them. Not everyone's as brave as you."

Sam knew he was joking because she wasn't brave at all. She just did what she wanted to do, even things that were hard for her, because that was better than not doing them at all.

"That's what brave means," whispered her dad, as if he knew what she was thinking.

Liam was still talking to Nelly. "Time to go home," his mom said gently, but the little brown dog rolled on her back, waving her paws for Liam to rub her speckly pink tummy.

"Nelly does love talking to little kids!" Mona laughed. "I bet she wishes she could go to school with you!"

Everyone laughed at Mona's joke, but at the back of Sam's mind, an idea started to grow.

Early Saturday morning, a young man turned up at the Rainbow Street Shelter holding a small brown-and-white guinea pig.

"I found this guy under a bush when I

took my dog out for a run," he said. "It was lucky the dog was on a leash, because she saw him before I did."

Nelly trotted out from behind the desk and sniffed the man's legs, looking up at the animal he was holding. The man held the guinea pig higher.

"It's okay," said Mona. "Nelly welcomes all the animals. They seem to know she wants to help them."

The man looked surprised but held the guinea pig a bit lower so Nelly could sniff. The guinea pig wiggled out of his hands, down to the floor.

"Oh, no!" shouted the man.

"No problem!" screeched Gulliver.

The white cat on the windowsill stopped halfway through combing the top of her head with her paws.

Mona shut the door to the outside runs. "It's okay," she said again, because Nelly had curled herself around the guinea pig, nuzzling and licking all over his body till the frightened animal stopped quivering.

"Do you have any idea where it might have escaped from?" Mona asked.

The man shook his head. "I asked everyone I saw. They all thought I was joking when I asked if they'd lost a guinea pig!"

"They can go farther than you'd think once they get loose," Mona said. "Now we just have to hope his owners think of looking for him here!"

"What happens if they don't?" asked the man.

"I'm sure we'll be able to find him a new home," said Mona. "But we'll wait for a week to give his owners a chance to find him first."

"Good luck, piggy!" said the man, and left.

Mona filled a small water dish and put it in front of the guinea pig. Then she got a cage ready in the small animal room, with clean hay and a little house for the guinea pig to hide in when he wanted.

"You can't stay out here loose in the waiting room," she told the lost animal, squatting down to pick him up. "You never know what big dog or cat might come in, and they're not all as nice as Nelly!"

She checked him over. He wasn't a baby, but he wasn't quite grown up yet.

"Poor little guy!" Mona murmured. "You're a bit thin, too. I think you might have been loose for a while."

But she couldn't find any cuts or sores;

his eyes and ears looked healthy, and so did his teeth.

"I think you'll be okay when you stop being so scared," Mona told him, placing him gently in the cage in the small animal room.

Nelly curled up at the front of the cage. The guinea pig stayed right where Mona had put him, just inside the door.

"Okay," said Mona. "If that's what you both want!"

She opened the door of the cage, and the little guinea pig nestled up to Nelly as if he was going home to his mother.

8

Liam's teacher was new. Sam had seen her when she met Liam at his classroom to go home from school, but she hadn't talked to her yet.

Sam always worried more about her words coming out wrong when she talked to someone for the first time. Especially when she was going to tell that person a crazy idea.

But maybe she wouldn't need to. Maybe Liam was so happy this week that Sam could drop her crazy idea before she even had to explain it to anyone.

The teacher smiled at Sam when she went to meet Liam on Monday afternoon.

"My brother's getting quite good at reading, isn't he?" Sam said.

She was hoping the teacher would say, "He sure is!" or "You must have given him lots of help for him to read so well already!"

But the teacher couldn't hear Sam wishing. "Don't worry," she said. "Lots of the kids are too shy to read out loud at the start of the year. It just takes them a while to warm up."

"He's not so shy when he talks to dogs," said Sam.

The teacher laughed, as if Sam had told a joke. "I'll remember that if I find a dog in my classroom one day!"

Sam decided she'd tell Mona her idea before she talked to the teacher—and first of all, she had to ask her parents.

Sam waited till Liam had gone to bed and she was alone with her mom and dad. "I know this sounds a bit crazy," she said.

"But you know how much Liam loves telling Nelly stories. What if he sometimes read to her instead of to the teacher? What if Nelly went to his class and all the kids got to read to her?"

"But—" said her mother.

"The teacher said lots of the kids are shy," Sam rushed on, before her mom could think exactly what the "but" was going to be. "So it would help all of them, not just Liam."

"Why do you want to do this so badly?" asked her dad.

Sam didn't know how to answer. Liam was her little brother, so of course she wanted him to be happy at school. She just didn't know exactly why it was so important to her that he should do things well.

"School wasn't very easy for you at the start, was it, Samantha?" asked her mom.

Sam shook her head. "No."

"You never told us," said her dad, "but we knew."

"I'd just like it to be nicer for Liam," said Sam.

"We'd have liked it to be nicer for you," said her dad.

"It's good now," said Sam.

"Okay," said her mom. "We'll go to see Mona tomorrow when I pick you up after school."

Mona was surprised when Mrs. Ballart, Sam, and Liam turned up at Rainbow Street again the next day.

"Is there a problem with Henry?" she asked.

"Henry's fine," said Sam. "Except he's probably a bit mad because I haven't gotten him out of his cage yet this afternoon."

She waited for her mom to tell Mona why they were there.

"Tell Mona your idea, Samantha," said her mom.

Liam was already sitting on the floor. He'd brought his school bag and was showing his book to Nelly.

It was the perfect way to explain what Sam meant. She took a deep breath.

"I wondered if Nelly could be a reader dog," she said.

"Sorry, but no!" said Mona.

Sam felt her brilliant idea shrivel and die. She'd known it was a bit crazy, but she hadn't thought Mona would say no so fast!

"Nelly's not for adoption," Mona went on. "She's mine, and the shelter's. She belongs here."

"I didn't mean all the time!" Sam protested. She thought about how she'd feel if someone wanted to take Henry away. She felt rude and mean that she'd ever had such a bad idea.

"I just wondered if you'd like to bring Nelly to visit the kindergarten kids so they could read to her."

"And that's the end of the story," Liam said to Nelly, and closed his book. Nelly licked him and rolled on her back for him to rub her pink freckled tummy.

Mona smiled. "That's a wonderful idea!" she said.

All the next morning, no matter what Sam's teacher was saying, all Sam could think about was what Liam's teacher would say that afternoon.

She might think Sam was crazy. She might laugh. She might hate dogs, or just say that it was against the rules.

At lunchtime, Hannah rushed over to Sam. Her ponytail was bouncing with excitement.

"I'm going to be a volunteer at the Rainbow Street Animal Shelter!" Hannah said. "I get to play with the dogs!"

Sam smiled. Everyone in the class knew how much Hannah loved dogs.

"How's your guinea pig?" Hannah asked, as if she'd suddenly remembered that dogs weren't the only pets in the world.

"He whistles when I come into the room," said Sam. "You can come and see him sometime if you want." And then she told Hannah her other idea.

"That is so cool!" said Hannah. "How did you come up with such an amazing plan?"

"The teacher might not think it's so amazing," Sam pointed out.

"Well, at first Mona and my parents thought I was too young to volunteer at the shelter," Hannah said. "Then Juan said he was probably too old, but if you added our ages up, we were both just right. So everybody gave in."

Sam laughed. She hoped she could be as brave as Hannah when she went to see Liam's teacher.

"A reading dog?" repeated Liam's teacher, when Sam told her. "What a fantastic idea!"

Sam beamed. She'd never thought it would be this easy!

"Of course it's not up to me," the teacher added. "You'll have to talk to Principal Stevens. It's too bad she's allergic to dogs."

The brown-and-white guinea pig had been eating busily all weekend, and already he wasn't quite so thin. He wasn't quite so nervous, either, and Nelly didn't think he needed her there all the time anymore. On Monday morning, she stayed with him for an hour or so, and then went back out to the waiting room to be with Mona and say hello to the other animals and people who came in.

But no one had phoned or come in to ask about a runaway guinea pig.

"Do you want me to go with you to talk to the principal?" Sam's mom asked that night.

Sam didn't want to go to see the principal one little bit. She was wishing she'd never thought of this crazy idea. Why did it even matter if her little brother wasn't brave at the start of kindergarten?

And if she did have to see the principal, she certainly didn't want to talk to her herself. The whole idea wouldn't sound nearly as crazy if her mom explained it.

"No, thanks," said Sam. "I'll do it myself."

So she started getting ready.

She looked up "reading dogs" online and found out that maybe this wasn't such a crazy idea after all. She printed out three articles and made a poster with a picture her mom had taken of Liam and Nelly pasted above the articles. Across the top she wrote in great big letters NELLY: THE READING DOG FOR OUR SCHOOL.

Then she lay on the rug in her bedroom, watching Henry roll a cardboard
tube across the floor. She didn't know if
he was trying to roll it or if he was trying
to chew it and it was rolling away. It didn't
matter: He was having fun, and she was
having fun watching him.

And the longer she watched him, and
especially when she held him against her
cheek before putting him back in his cage
for the night, the happier she felt.

Suddenly a little voice in her head said that maybe there was a simpler way to make Liam happier and braver.

Sam didn't want to listen to that little voice. Liam could do lots of things; having a guinea pig was a special thing that was just hers. She did not want to share it.

9

It was a busy morning at the Rainbow Street Shelter. Mona's phone was ringing before she'd even had time to unlock the cherry red front door.

"I can hear a kitten meowing in the garden," said the woman on the other end of the phone. "But I can't find it, and I've got to go to work in an hour."

"I'll be there soon as I can," said Mona, opening the door. Blanco was stepping out of her basket under the desk, meowing and stretching. Nelly rushed in to greet her, then into the small animal room to check her guinea pig, and finally into the hospital room to see a dog who'd come in with a broken leg the day before.

"Can I help you?" Gulliver was screeching from his perch above the desk.

Mona checked the hospital animals and gave the dog a shot to keep the broken leg from hurting. Nelly licked the dog's face while Mona gave him the shot.

"*Hola, amigo!*" Gulliver shrieked, and Juan came in.

"I think Nelly helps as much as the

medicine!" he said, rubbing the little dog's head.

Mona told him about the lost kitten. "I'll take Nelly with me," she said.

She drove out to the woman's house, and Nelly helped her search the garden. It didn't take the little stumpy-tailed dog long to find five tiny kittens, so new their eyes were still shut. She started licking them right away. They were chilly and weak, and Nelly knew that if they didn't get warm soon, they could die.

"You're right, Nelly," said Mona, as she nestled the kittens into a soft towel in the bottom of a cat carry cage. "I don't know what happened to their mom, but these little guys are really missing her!"

"What if she comes back?" asked the woman who'd phoned.

"Call us right away," said Mona. "But it looks to me like they've been here for a while on their own. The most important thing now is to get them back to the shelter and get some milk into them."

The woman touched one of the tiny heads with her finger. "I really don't want a cat," she said, but she didn't sound very sure, and when she rushed away to work, she had tears in her eyes.

"Wouldn't surprise me if you see her again when you're bigger," Mona told the kittens, and loaded the carry case into the station wagon.

When they got back to the shelter, Juan and Mona fed the kittens with a special kitty bottle and then put them into a box where Nelly nuzzled and licked them clean and warm. The abandoned kittens nestled up against her, purring gently.

At lunchtime, when everyone else in the class was going out to play, Sam went to see Principal Stevens. Her stomach was tied up in a tight knot, and she was afraid her tongue might be, too. Her hand didn't want to knock on the office door.

But somehow it did, and when Principal Stevens told her to come in, Sam's legs did what they were told—and then there was nothing she could do but explain her idea.

"You know how some little kids don't like reading out loud because they think people are going to laugh at them?"

The principal nodded.

Sam held up her Reading Dog poster. "If they read to a dog, they might get braver, because dogs never laugh at you."

"That's true," said the principal.

"I know a dog who's so gentle that she even looks after sick animals, and she *loves* little kids! And Mona at the Rainbow Street Shelter said she could bring her here once a week to visit the kindergarten class."

"That's a very good idea!" Principal Stevens said.

Sam took a deep breath. She'd been just about to explain all about the shelter, and now she didn't know what to do with all those words crowding to get out.

"I thought you were allergic!" Sam said instead. And then she turned red, because that didn't sound like the sort of thing you were supposed to say to a principal.

"I am," said Principal Stevens. "And some kids may be, too. There'll be lots of details to sort out, but it's a great idea, and I think we should try."

10

The very next week, Mona started taking Nelly to the kindergarten class for a visit every Friday afternoon, and for that first time, Sam was invited, too.

A special corner was set up with a comfy mat for the little stumpy-tailed dog. The kids took turns going up to the mat with their books and plopping down beside her. Sam and Mona sat in chairs behind the mat, close enough that Mona was there for Nelly, but not so close that they seemed to be listening to the story.

Liam went first. He nestled himself down beside the little dog and showed her his reader, pointing out the pictures and making up the story when he didn't know the words. He read so loudly and clearly that Mona and Sam could hear every word, and his teacher smiled in surprise.

When the story was finished, Nelly rolled on her back and let him rub her freckled pink tummy for a minute, and then it was someone else's turn to read.

She listened to every child as if she couldn't believe how lucky she was, and as if each story was the best she'd ever heard. She didn't laugh when they said words wrong, and she didn't correct them when they didn't know what the words were. Nelly just let them tell the story the way they wanted.

A few kids didn't even try to read, but they whispered secrets against her warm fur—and Nelly licked their sadness away, just like she cleaned little puppies and kittens.

Sam watched the kids' faces get happier and braver as they sat with the little dog. She saw how they stood up taller when they went back to their desks after rubbing the freckled pink tummy. She completely forgot that she'd felt a bit strange at first, sitting in a chair in the little kids' class, and started to feel as warm and happy as when she cuddled Henry.

Mona was smiling, too, and Sam knew that she was feeling exactly the same way.

The teacher asked the children to thank Mona and Nelly as they left.

"And let's thank Samantha for organizing this, too," she added.

Liam jumped up and hugged his sister. All the other little kids followed him, jumping around Sam in a giant group hug that nearly knocked her over.

"Thank you!" they squealed.

Sam felt as warm as if she'd stepped into a hot, bubbly bath. Even though she'd talked about other kids when she told the grown-ups her plan, she'd really just been thinking about her own little brother. She'd never thought about all the kids who

were going to be just as happy as Liam.
She hadn't known it would make her feel
so good.

Henry was dozing inside his guinea pig
palace. He couldn't be bothered to climb
his ramp or play in his hay, because there
was no one to share it or watch him. It
didn't matter how loudly he chirruped or
where he explored; he was alone.

It was Mr. Ballart's turn to pick up Sam
and Liam from school. "I think we should
celebrate Sam's great idea!" he said. "I've
got your bathing suits and towels. How

about we make the most of this warm weather and go straight to the beach, then meet your mom for dinner?"

Mrs. Ballart's office was in a tall building right downtown. They walked around the corner to a restaurant with candles on the tables. Sam had spaghetti and fruit salad with ice cream for dessert.

"This is one of the best days of my life!" said Sam.

"Me too!" said Liam.

It was late when they went home. Liam fell sound asleep in the car, and Sam nearly did, too. She was ready to tumble into her bed and dream about her big day.

But as she was about to open her bedroom door, there was a rustling and whistling. Henry was standing up against the side of his hutch, waiting for his play-time and treats.

"Oh, Henry!" said Sam. "I forgot all about you!"

She picked him up and cuddled him against her chin. Henry wiggled—he wanted to get down on the floor and run around.

"Straight to bed, Sam!" called her mom.

"But Henry's lonely!" Sam protested.

"You can talk to him in the morning," said her mom.

All Sam could do was sneak in a piece of celery for Henry to eat in his cage and go to bed. But she knew she wouldn't be dreaming about her wonderful day; the warm bubble-bath feeling had all drained away.

She couldn't believe she'd forgotten about her little friend.

11

"I've been thinking," said Sam the next morning. "It's not fair for Henry to be all alone in his cage when I don't come home to play with him."

"You can't stay home all the time to look after a guinea pig!" said her dad.

"That's not what I mean," said Sam.

Sam took an apple back for Henry while she waited for her parents to talk about her idea. She let Henry roll it from one side of her room to the other. She opened up a big brown paper bag for him to crawl inside and explore.

"I'll never let you be lonely again!" she whispered.

"Sam!" her dad called.

Sam picked up Henry. The guinea pig was happy now that he'd gotten to play and whuffled quietly under Sam's chin as she went back to the kitchen.

"Are you sure about this?" her dad asked.

"I'm sure," said Sam.

"Look, Nelly!" Mona called as the Ballarts came in the cherry red door. "Here are some of your favorite people!"

Nelly trotted out from where she'd

been snuggling with the kittens and rushed to Liam.

"She's been really happy since we visited the school," Mona told Sam. "And how's Henry?"

"He's lonely," said Sam.

"We might be able to help you with that," said Mona. "Nelly!" she called. "Let's show everyone the new piggy."

Nelly led them into the small animal room, where the little brown-and-white guinea pig was sitting in his hutch.

"He hasn't been claimed, so he's ready to go to a new home today," Mona said, as she opened the door and picked up the guinea pig. "He's young, so he and Henry should get along. But you still have to be sure you can love him, too."

She put him into Sam's arms.

"He's not for me," said Sam. And she gave the guinea pig to her brother.

Liam's eyes opened wide with surprise. He was too excited to speak as the guinea pig scrambled up against his chest.

Nelly licked them both until the guinea pig and the boy knew she'd made them belong together.

"What's his name?" Liam asked at last.

"He's waiting for you to tell him," said Mona.

"Gingersnap," said Liam.

When they got home, they put a beach towel on the living room floor. Sam sat at one end with Henry, and Liam sat at the other end with Gingersnap. After a while, they put their guinea pigs down.

Gingersnap stayed close to Liam. Henry started to explore the new room, and then stopped and sniffed. He could smell a new guinea pig, and he was deciding whether it was a friend or an enemy.

Henry stomped toward Gingersnap. His hackles were up to make him look bigger, and he held his nose high in the air.

Gingersnap quivered so he looked even smaller. He put his nose down low.

Henry sniffed him all over, then scampered off across the floor, looking behind

him as if asking his new friend if he
wanted to follow.

When it was time to put them both into
the guinea pig palace between Sam's and
Liam's rooms, Henry flipped and pop-
corned for joy, up and down the ramp, and
all over the cage.

After a little while, Gingersnap did, too.

How did the Rainbow Street Shelter begin?

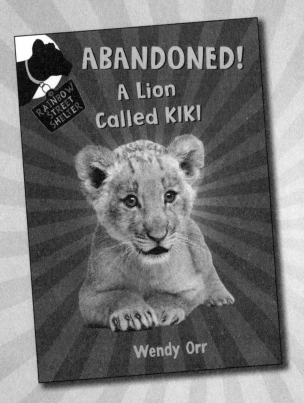

ABANDONED!
A Lion
Called KIKI

RAINBOW STREET SHELTER

Wendy Orr

Find out what happens when Mona is gifted with her first real animal . . . a baby lion.

Mona's attic bedroom in Grammie and
Grandpa's house looked just the way she'd
remembered it from last summer. The
bedspread was patterned with ducklings,
and an old teddy bear that had been her
dad's was on the pillow. An envelope was
propped up on the bear's scruffy paws.

Inside it were three tickets to the circus and a note:

Happy early birthday!
   These tickets include
a behind-the-scenes tour to
see Amazing, Fearsome, and Cute
Animals with your favorite uncle.
   See you Sunday!
      Love,
      Uncle Matthew

Uncle Matthew was Mona's dad's younger brother. Except for their red hair and bright blue eyes, they were as different as two brothers could be. Mona's father worked in an office and was always worried, but Uncle Matthew was a juggler in a circus and never worried about anything.

The circus traveled all over the country. Mona and her parents had seen it in their city the winter before. They'd watched Uncle Matthew juggle small bright balls and long striped batons. And when all the lights in the big top went off, Mona knew that the person in the middle of the ring, tossing flaming torches high into the blackness, was her very own uncle Matthew.

Early on Sunday morning, Mona's mother and father took a taxi back to the airport. Mona wouldn't see them again until the end of the summer. For a minute, she felt very alone.

Then Grammie's hand, warm and comforting, wrapped around hers. Buck, the sort-of border collie, nosed her a ball to throw, and Grandpa said, "Four more hours till the circus!"

Excitement chased the loneliness right out of her body.

It was the best circus Mona had ever seen. Clowns tumbled, poodles rolled barrels, and Uncle Matthew, juggling silvery rings, danced on tall stilts. The lion trainer cracked his whip, and the lion roared back, his tail swishing angrily. The McNeils'

seats were so close they could see his pink tongue and sharp, pointed teeth.

Mona shivered, held her breath, and clapped till her hands were sore—but she never quite stopped wondering what she was going to see after the show.

Finally, when the rest of the audience was going home, full to the brim with amazement and popcorn, Uncle Matthew tapped Mona on the shoulder.

Mona and her grandparents followed him out of the big top, past the other tents and trailers, to one that smelled of hay and animals.

"Keep very quiet," said the lion trainer as Uncle Matthew led Mona and her grandparents in.

A lioness was lying on the floor of a big cage, with four tiny cubs snuggled against her. She lifted her head and snarled at the strangers. Mona shivered. She didn't need the lion trainer to tell her they shouldn't go any closer.

The cubs were about as big as guinea pigs, with spotty golden brown fur. Their eyes were shut tight; they were blind and helpless, and Mona wanted to hold one more than she'd ever wanted anything in her whole life. She could nearly feel how soft and sweet they'd be to cuddle. It was hard to believe they were going to grow up to be fierce, roaring lions.

But the lioness was glaring, her teeth

and eyes bright in the darkness as she warned them all to keep away from her cubs. All Mona could do was stand outside the cage and think how she would love them if she only had the chance.

Amy lives and breathes horses, but all her horses are in books or in her head. When she goes on a picnic and hears a neigh, it's a dream come true. But what's a horse doing in the park?

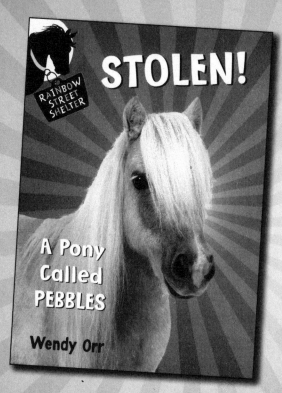

With Mona's help, Amy cares for the horse. Amy almost hopes the owner never turns up so she can keep visiting the pony. . . .

1

The stables on the hill were shadowed and quiet in the moonlight. As the two men in dark clothes crept down the long hall, they could smell the warm scent of clean horses and fresh hay.

"Go right to the end," whispered the leader.

They snuck into the last stall, where Pebbles was sleeping. She was short and stocky, silvery white with some darker gray dapples across her rump. Her eyes were soft and brown in her pretty face.

"That's not a racehorse!" the smaller thief snarled. "We're in the wrong stall!"

A tall black stallion sprang to his feet. The men heard his hooves strike the floor. They felt the rush of his powerful body, and now that their eyes were used to the darkness, they saw his shape.

"*That's* Midnight!" exclaimed the boss thief. Before the stallion knew what was happening, a rope had been thrown around his neck and looped over his nose into a halter.

The horse's eyes rolled white with fear and rage. He jerked back and reared, his strong front legs slashing the air. The thief holding the halter was thrown into the corner of the stall. He rolled out of the way just as Midnight's hooves thudded down.

"Forget it!" the smaller man screamed. "I'm not going to get killed just to steal a horse!"

"Be quiet!" said the boss thief. He opened the stall door and pushed the other man out.

The stallion pawed the floor, snorting in alarm.

The thief ignored him. He rubbed the silver mare between her ears and breathed gently into her nostrils.

"What are you doing?" the smaller man demanded. "That's not the one we want!"

"I'm guessing this big guy doesn't go anywhere without his little friend. And when you're worth as much as he is, what you want is what you get."

The boss slipped a rope halter over Pebbles's head.

2

Amy had wanted a horse for as long as she could remember. She liked ponies, but what she really wanted was a horse. She drew horses, painted horses, watched horse shows, and collected horse books, horse ornaments, and horse pictures. She wanted a horse so badly that sometimes she pretended she *was* one. When she ran barefoot on the lawn, she imagined that her feet were hooves striking the ground. She practiced trotting with her knees high and cantering fast and smooth, with her left leg leading.

Other times, she pretended that her bike was a horse, except that she had to do the pedaling.

But mostly she imagined what it would be like to have her own horse. She would brush its big body and comb its long mane. She would look into its eyes and climb on its back, and ride it everywhere.

"Amy," her mom always said, "you know we can't have a horse. Horses are expensive—and where would we keep it?"